PET HOTEL

Any creature that leaps, runs, flies or swims
is welcome at Tangletrees Pet Hotel...

Have you read all the

PET HOTEL

books?

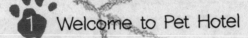
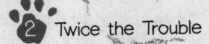
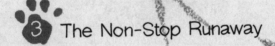

More
Pet Hotel animal stories
out soon!

2

Twice
the
Trouble

Sara Carroll

BBC

First published in 1998 by BBC Worldwide Ltd
Woodlands, 80 Wood Lane, London W12 0TT

Text by Sara Carroll copyright © BBC Worldwide Ltd 1998
The author asserts the moral right to be identified as the author of the work.

Girl Talk copyright © BBC Worldwide Ltd 1995

ISBN 0 563 380 95 0

Cover and inside illustrations by Penny Ives
copyright © BBC Worldwide Ltd 1998

Printed and bound by Mackays of Chatham plc

Contents

1

Monday Morning Surprise

"Becky, look! It's amazing!"

Becky Ashford sleepily turned over and looked at her bedside clock. It was eight o'clock. On a normal Monday morning she would be in school by now, but not today. This was the first morning of half term and her dad was letting her have a lie in. Her younger sister, Sophie, however, seemed to have other ideas.

"Come on, wake up! It's incredible outside!" Sophie shook her, then jumped on the bed as she sang:

"*Snow had fallen, snow on snow!*

Snow on snow

In the bleak midwinter..."

"Sophie," grumbled Becky. "What are you *on* about? Christmas was over weeks ago."

"Sorry!" beamed Sophie. "But what would you sing about weather like this? *Look!"* She flung open the curtains with a theatrical swish.

It did look beautiful outside. The trees were coated in a thick layer of glistening white and despite how lovely and cosy it was under the duvet, Becky got up and joined her sister.

"Wow! We never had snow like this in London."

"I know!" grinned Sophie. "And I'm going to be the first to get my wellies on and go out in it!"

With that, Sophie marched out of the room, singing as she went.

As Becky reached for her dressing gown and wiggled her toes into her slippers, Albert, their West Highland Terrier, trotted into the room.

"Hello, Bertie," she said, kneeling down to scratch him behind the ears. "What do you think of all this snow, then?" But the little white Westie just put his paws up on her knees and panted for more scratching. "I wish Sophie was as quiet as you, sometimes!" she whispered with a smile. By the sound of things, Sophie had started singing again in the kitchen and Dan Ashford, her dad, had joined in.

"Just listen to them!" Becky sighed. "Come on, let's go and get some breakfast."

"Hi, Dad."

"Morning, Becks!" Her father kissed her on the forehead, then carried on making up silly songs.

"Jingle bells, jingle bells,

Jingle all the way.

Oh what fun we're going to have

At Tangletrees today. Hey!"

Tangletrees Pet Hotel was the animal holiday centre Dan had set up with their good friend and great animal lover, Angela Fitzgerald. She had started off as the girls' childminder, but talked

Dan into giving up his city job and helping her turn her huge old house into a kennels for all types of pets.

"I wonder if we'll have any interesting guests over half term," said Becky over breakfast.

"We'll certainly have an interesting time if this weather keeps up," replied Dan. "Now, apart from mucking out, shovelling snow and making tea for me and Mrs Fitz, what do you two fancy doing over half term? I thought it might be fun to try out the Clayton ice-rink."

"Ooh, can we?" squeaked Sophie.

"Well, *you* can. I think I'll just sit and have a nice coffee at the side."

"Brilliant, Dad!" added Becky.

"And can I invite Isabel over to Tangletrees, Dad?" asked Sophie. Isabel was her best friend — they'd met when the sisters had started at St Sebastian's last term.

"Sure! And you need some new jeans, Becks. Perhaps we could combine the ice-skating with a shopping trip."

Becky's face lit up again. "This is going to be an *excellent* half term!"

"Why don't you ring a friend to help you choose?" suggested Dan.

Becky concentrated hard on pouring out some cereal. She hadn't found a friend as quickly as Sophie had found Isabel, but she wasn't keen on letting her dad know this in case he worried. The one person she really liked at school was Amy, who she'd got to know when they were on hamster duty together. The bad news was that Amy was in Deborah's gang, a group of girls in her class who stuck together and were suspicious of newcomers. In the eyes of Deborah Porter, their leader, Becky was an outsider. She seemed to go out of her way to make Becky feel unwanted, particularly by saying cruel and untrue things about Pet Hotel.

Becky was saved from answering by the front doorbell.

"Postman!" yelled Sophie as she galloped off to answer it. She came back, brushing snow off a large envelope. "It's from Mum!"

Becky and Sophie cheered. Their parents had divorced just before they'd moved down to Haresfield, and while Dan looked after them, their mum, Sarah, was now living in France. Shovelling in the last mouthful of breakfast, Becky pushed her bowl away as Sophie opened the package and produced three more envelopes — a letter for each of them. The family read them together, enjoying the chatty details and stories. Becky and Sophie read out bits to each other, whooping and laughing. Letters from their mum were the best way to start half term.

"OK, you lot!" Dan announced, eventually. "Some people have to go to work today and Mrs Fitz will not be pleased with me if I miss the morning chores, so hurry up. The chariot departs in fifteen minutes. Put on plenty of warm clothes, and don't forget your hat this time, Soph."

By some miracle the Ashfords were all in the car fifteen minutes later, including Albert. By another miracle, the car eventually started.

"I think this old thing needs a visit to the garage," sighed Dan as he backed out of the drive at April Close. "I don't fancy breaking down in this weather."

"It just needs a rest!" cried Sophie. "Maybe we could start a car hotel too!"

Although most of the main roads round the village had been cleared, they were still very slippery. It took twice as long as usual to get to Tangletrees. But the instant Albert worked out where they were, the Westie started snuffling excitedly.

"Hey, is that Mrs Fitz?" asked Becky.

"Can't see," squealed Sophie, winding down her window. "Yes!" she yelled. "Morning!"

A figure waved back to them. It was Mrs Fitzgerald — dressed from head to toe in various shades of purple. She had been scattering sand from a large plastic bucket onto the drive, but stopped as soon as she recognised their car and waved energetically.

"Whoops!"

"Oh no!" shrieked Becky, as Mrs Fitzgerald lost her balance and fell over backwards, sending the bucket flying. The next minute, all they could see was a pair of green boots waving in the air.

Dan stopped the car quickly and the two girls leapt out. "Careful of the ice!" he called. "We don't want any more slip-ups!"

2

Here Comes Trouble!

"Spot the idiot!" groaned Mrs Fitzgerald as the girls arrived. "What did I think I was doing, waving like that?"

"Are you OK?" asked Becky, bending down to pick up one of Mrs Fitz's pink gloves that had gone flying.

"Bruised from top to toe, but apart from that I'm fine. Would you believe it, the wretched bucket bounced off my head. That's what hurts the most."

"You really all right, Angela?" called Dan as he

joined them.

"Of course. I just need a hand up!"

Dan and the two girls helped her to stand — and only then did they take in exactly what she was wearing. Mrs Fitzgerald caught sight of their surprised looks.

"What do you think?" she held her arms out and did a careful little twirl. "I am modelling the new keep-warm-at-all-costs range."

Under an old purple anorak drooped a very long and saggy purple jumper. Round her neck was a huge crocheted scarf, purple of course, and on her head no less than two woolly hats.

"It's…" began Becky. "It's very…"

"It's very *purple*," concluded Sophie, weakly.

Mrs Fitz grinned. "Do you know, I'm growing to like it! Where's *your* hat, Sophie?"

Sophie looked sheepish.

"Not again?" groaned Dan.

"Good job I've got two!" said Mrs Fitzgerald, plonking a bright purple woollen thing on Sophie's head.

"That looks like a tea cosy!" laughed Becky.

They began to walk towards the house. "Now that the fashion show's over, how are our guests doing?" said Dan with a smile.

"*They're* all fine. I think it's us humans who have such trouble with the cold — I can't remember Haresfield ever being this freezing before."

"Can we have a cup of hot chocolate before we start, Mrs Fitz?" asked Sophie, cheekily. "I mean, it *is* really cold…"

"I don't see why not," said Mrs Fitzgerald indulgently. "Everything's running a bit late this morning. The phone hasn't stopped ringing — new guests mostly and Donald Hall checking I wasn't snowed in…" Mr Hall was in charge of the local vet's practice, and his advice on animal care was invaluable to the team at Pet Hotel.

They followed her through the back door, leaving their snowy boots in the porch as they passed.

Pet Hotel was busy this half-term. Its reputation had spread, and the centre was taking in animals from many of the surrounding towns and villages. At the moment their guests included a host of rabbits, guinea pigs, hamsters and gerbils; several budgies, plus at least a dozen cats and dogs. They even had a hibernating tortoise and a tank of stick insects in residence! Dan, Mrs Fitzgerald and the girls were thrilled that Tangletrees had become so popular.

Sophie and Becky began their chores on the first floor with the small animals, checking the recent care charts and ticking off each cage as they changed the straw and fed the occupants.

Mrs Fitzgerald hovered about as they worked. "We need to keep a careful eye on Henry the hamster over there. He hasn't moved from his little house — perhaps he's a bit depressed."

"I'm off to look at those two rabbit hutches we bought at the boot fair last week," said Dan, laden with new bedding from the first floor storeroom. "They could go rotten in this weather."

"Grand idea," said Mrs Fitzgerald.

"And if you're really good, Dad, we'll make

you a nice mug of hot chocolate later," said Becky, smiling at him.

"Just in time to welcome the Hardys at eleven," muttered Mrs Fitz, trying not to sound too sour.

"The Hardys?" queried Dan, in the doorway. "I didn't know we were dealing with them."

"*Who's* coming today?" asked Sophie, who had been distracted while she stroked a gerbil through its open cage.

"Mr and Mrs Hardy — they're bringing their two Cocker spaniels," said Mrs Fitzgerald with a sigh.

There was an awkward silence. Mr Hardy was a wealthy landowner from Clayton, the town about eight kilometres away. He was trying very hard to buy the land opposite Tangletrees to develop into a leisure complex which, as far as everyone had heard, would include late-night parties and discos. He had built a similar complex just outside Clayton and they were all horrified to think he might put something like that opposite Pet Hotel. It would disturb their peace and people might be put off from boarding their pets next to a place teeming with cars and loud music.

Mrs Fitzgerald had already looked into buying the land herself, but it was too expensive. Instead, she was making it her mission to let everyone know what he was up to and to try to stop him.

"We've got a Siamese cat coming later on too," Mrs Fitzgerald called out, brightly, but Dan had closed the door behind him without another word. Mrs Fitz sighed again, and turned to Sophie and Becky. "I've had a pile of leaflets printed, by the way, outlining Hardy's plans. Perhaps you two wouldn't mind helping me deliver them?"

Becky nodded seriously, but Sophie let out a yelp.

"Aargh! He's gone down my jumper!" The gerbil Sophie had been stroking had zoomed up her arm.

"Stay still a minute," the old lady said as she reached down Sophie's back. "Poor thing! Can't be much fun in there!"

"Oooh!" screeched Sophie. "It's itching like mad!"

"Got him!" Mrs Fitzgerald expertly scooped up the gerbil and placed him back in his cage. "Shall I handle the cage? *I'm* not ticklish."

It took well over an hour to look in on all the animals, giving each one a stroke and making sure they felt at home. The girls were just putting away the charts when they heard a car pull up the drive. Sophie rushed to the window to see who it was.

"Fat man with glasses and thin lady with red hair," she announced.

"Don't be so rude," chuckled Mrs Fitzgerald. "However, that sounds distinctly like Mr and Mrs Hardy!"

Mrs Fitzgerald put the last of the charts away. "Well, I suppose I'd better go and meet them." She opened the door just as the couple were climbing the front steps.

"Ah, Mrs Fitzgerald. Here are my lovely dogs, just as I promised," said Mr Hardy. "This one is Whisky... Here boy... and that one is Ginger!" As he spoke, Ginger pulled away from her master and bounced up to Mrs Fitzgerald, nearly knocking her over with the force of her greeting. Whisky thought this looked like great fun, and joined in. The pair of spaniels worked themselves into a frenzy, jumping and yapping all over the place.

"Please, Mr Hardy," protested Mrs Fitzgerald. "Kindly keep your dogs under control!"

With a yelp of horror, Mrs Fitzgerald's ginger cats, who had been lying peacefully under the radiator in the entrance hall, raced upstairs. Sophie, however, dashed over to stroke the spaniels. Whisky was black and the bigger of the two, while Ginger was, as her name suggested, a lovely ginger-brown.

Mrs Hardy smiled sweetly at Sophie. "Yes, they are gorgeous. I'll miss them terribly while we're away."

"They'll be really happy here, I promise," said Sophie, patting them affectionately.

"Perhaps, Mr and Mrs Hardy, you could follow me?" asked Mrs Fitzgerald. She glanced at the spaniels. "And if you call your dogs to order we'll be able to get through the official bit so much faster!"

Mr Hardy laughed. "I'll do my best!" he said, although it was a good five minutes before they had calmed down enough to follow their owners into the office.

But it didn't last long. Mr Hardy was constantly trying to command them to heel, but they seemed totally out of control. The pair even grabbed the Pet Hotel contract from out of his hand and began chewing it. Just when it seemed there would be more paper on the floor than on the desk, Sophie piped up, "Shall we hold the dogs for you?"

"That sounds a *very* good idea!" said Mrs Fitzgerald, nodding briskly.

Finally, when the paperwork was completed

and the dogs taken to their pen, the Hardys turned to go. Mrs Fitzgerald extended a hand which, to her surprise, Mr Hardy grasped warmly.

"Thank you, Mrs Fitzgerald. I can see our dogs are in excellent hands. Whisky and Ginger are lucky pups."

"Yes," said Mrs Fitzgerald, tightly. "Aren't they."

"See you in a week!" he called as they opened the door, Mrs Hardy raising a gloved hand to wave.

"He's got a nerve!" puffed Mrs Fitzgerald, when they'd gone. " I could have guessed *his* dogs would be a handful."

"Well, I like lively dogs," said Sophie.

"There's a big difference between lively dogs and disobedient dogs, which is what these are. Oh dear, I *do* hope they don't cause us too much trouble!"

Becky and Sophie exchanged looks. It was already shaping up to be an interesting week.

3

The Arrival of Lady Jane

Becky trudged out to the stables to groom Billy, Mrs Fitzgerald's Shetland pony. It was her favourite job at Tangletrees, and she did it every day, even when she was at school. Becky was beginning to think of Billy as her own pony.

The Shetland trotted over as soon as he saw Becky striding across the snowy meadow. She patted his chestnut-coloured head. "Good boy. You come when you're called, don't you — not like our latest guests!"

Little Albert barked as if agreeing with her. The Westie ploughed through the snow, in and out of Billy's legs.

Becky laughed. "You see, Billy? Even Bertie's had enough of Whisky and Ginger! And I don't think Charlie's very pleased to see them either." Charlie was Mrs Fitz's own golden retriever and had become Bertie's best friend at Tangletrees.

Billy snickered quietly as Becky carried on telling him about the dogs, gently brushing the pony's mane and coat. It seemed as if he was really enjoying the story. "There — you'll do!" With a final pat and a hug, she led Billy back to his stable and draped his winter rug over him.

THUD!

A huge snowball landed at her feet. She looked up just in time to glimpse Sophie's head disappearing round the corner.

"Hey, you! Watch out, you could scare Billy!" But Sophie wasn't listening. She was sprinting off up the paddock to get away. "Come on, Bertie, let's get her back!" Making sure the stable door was closed, Becky chased after her sister.

It was a spectacular snowball fight. Both girls fell over several times, often when Bertie skidded into them in the snow, yelping with excitement as he chased between them. Soon, the girls were pink-cheeked and puffing.

Out of breath from laughing so much, they had just called a truce when they spotted a black Jaguar pull up in the driveway. Becky stopped in her tracks when she saw who got out — a tall, elegant lady and a young girl. It was Deborah Porter from her class, and the woman, carrying a large wicker cat basket, had to be her mother. So it was *Deborah's* Siamese who was checking in!

"Let's just go and see Billy," she said to Sophie,

27

hastily. She had seen Deborah's expensive jacket and stylish felt hat, and didn't want to be caught in her wellies, old duffle coat and woolly bobble hat drooping with snow.

"I thought you just did that!" protested Sophie. "Anyway, I'm soaking wet, and Dad will give us an earful if he catches us out here like this."

Becky knew Sophie was right, and so decided to confess to her sister. "Wait, Soph. That girl's in my class and I don't want her to see me like this. Let's stay out of sight for a minute — *please*?"

"Oh, OK," nodded Sophie, puzzled. "Why don't we go and wait behind the door at the top of the basement stairs. They won't see us there *and* we can hear what they say!"

Becky nodded. "Good idea, Soph! Come on!"

"You see Mr...?"

"Ashford," the girls heard their dad say.

"Well, Mr *Ashforth*, I am not a great fan of kennels and such places — they're full of disease and frequently staffed by untrained amateurs."

"Cheek!" whispered Sophie, but Becky shushed her.

"However, this is an emergency," Mrs Porter went on. "My mother has 'flu and I simply *must* go and see her. I couldn't find anyone to feed Lady Jane at such short notice."

"Lady Jane?" Dan's voice rose again.

"Deborah's cat."

"Oh. I wondered if you meant your daughter, for a minute, there!"

Becky winced, but Sophie giggled. "Nice one, Dad!"

"Ssh, Sophie!" hissed Becky, furiously.

"It's just that I have two girls of my own so I'm sure we could cope!" Dan continued, laughing.

'Please shut up, Dad,' thought Becky.

Mrs Porter just ignored him. "Now, she is rather a special cat, and we only feed her freshly-cooked meat. She also enjoys a little chocolate after dinner."

"Chocolate!" gasped Sophie. Becky covered her sister's mouth with her hand. They heard their dad reply.

"This is the list of foods we give the cats that stay. She will have fresh food twice a week, but we do prefer to give them the recommended combination of dried and tinned foods."

"Oh dear," came Mrs Porter's sniffy voice. "Well, I suppose this will have to do…"

"I just need you to sign a few forms," said Dan, brightly. "So, if you'd like to come into the office…"

Becky could just see her dad through the window of the basement door as he walked off. She realised in horror that he was still in his smelly old wellies and what he called his 'worst' outdoor coat. She saw Deborah following behind, her nose firmly in the air — held as far away from the wellies as possible, Becky guessed.

As they pressed against the door, the sisters could just hear Deborah speaking.

"We've put her favourite velvet cushion in here, and this is her brush for her daily care routine. I usually call her just Lady, and she should answer to that if you call her."

Becky couldn't hold Sophie quiet any longer.

"Velvet cushion!" she spluttered, and there was a silence from the office. Had they heard Sophie or were they just filling out the forms?

Sophie started poking Becky in the ribs.

"Hey, stop it," whispered Becky. But Sophie carried on until Becky nudged her with her elbow, sending her tumbling out from behind the door.

"Ow!" yelled Sophie. Becky squashed herself flatter against the wall, praying she was out of sight.

"Sophie! Where did you spring from?" she heard Dan say.

"Er — the basement," she said quickly.

"In a wet coat? I'd go and change if I were you. This is my youngest daughter, Mrs Porter. Becky must be around somewhere. Have you seen her, Soph?"

Becky held her breath.

"No, Dad. Probably out with Billy or something."

Becky heard her sister thunder up the stairs. "Nice one, Sophie!" she breathed.

As soon as the Porters were gone Becky emerged

to have a look at Deborah's precious cat. Dan was just taking her to a cage.

"Hello! Another mysteriously appearing daughter who looks like a drowned rat!" laughed Dan.

Becky peered at Lady. "Bit stuck-up looking, Siamese cats, aren't they?"

"I do prefer Tabbies myself," agreed Dan. "But she's obviously a much-loved pet."

"You'd have to be a bit stuck-up yourself to have a Siamese, don't you think?"

"I'm not sure that's a very nice thing to say, Becky." He frowned as he caught sight of Becky's troubled expression. "What's all this about, love?"

"Deborah Porter is in my class at school."

"And?"

"Well..." Becky hesitated, unsure whether to tell her dad what was going on. She wished her mum was around.

"Come on, Becks," said Dan, coaxingly.

Becky took a deep breath. "She doesn't really like me, I don't know why. I tried to be friends with her, but... Dad, she's said some horrid things about Pet Hotel."

Dan sighed. "You should have told me about this if it's bothering you — it's always better to talk these things through, Becks." His face softened. "Anyway, now you *have* told me, I'd say this is the ideal opportunity to show her how *good* we are. Who knows, this could be the turning point — you might end up the best of friends!"

Becky doubted it, but she smiled at her dad anyway as he put his arm round her shoulders.

"Besides," he continued, "I'm not sure how much she knows about pets if she's feeding her cat chocolate every day. Now hurry up and change into some dry clothes before you soak me, too!"

At the end of the day the girls went round to say goodnight to all the animals. Becky thought she ought to just look in on Lady Jane. The cat was sitting there on her velvet cushion ignoring everyone, her twitching nose at just the same angle as Deborah's had been earlier. Becky felt irritated. Here was a constant reminder of the one person she was trying to forget this week. But her thoughts were broken by Sophie pulling her arm.

"Let's go and say goodnight to the spaniels," her little sister said. "Come on."

Becky allowed herself to be pulled away. Whisky and Ginger were overjoyed to see them — so overjoyed that there was a minor accident. As Whisky nuzzled Sophie through the cage he couldn't control himself any longer and the girls could only watch as a large puddle formed on the floor of his pen.

Their giggling brought Mrs Fitzgerald and Dan to see what was going on. Mrs Fitz smiled and went for the mop. "Oh dear," they heard her say from the cupboard. "I was hoping this pair might settle down, but perhaps it was wishful thinking!"

4

Dog Discipline

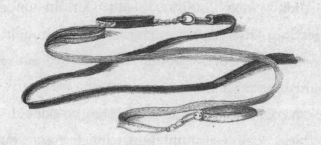

The phone was ringing as Dan and the girls arrived home that evening.

"Quick, Dad!" urged Becky as her father fumbled with the key in the lock.

The second it was open Sophie ducked under his arm and charged to the phone yelling, "Don't hang up!" Bertie hared after her, yapping wildly as she grabbed the receiver. "Hello?" she gasped, out of breath.

"Is that Sophie? It's Donald Hall, here."

"Hi, Mr Hall! I'll get Dad," answered Sophie. Becky peeled off her fleece, trying not to show her disappointment. She'd secretly hoped it might be her mum, Sarah.

Dan took the phone. "Hello, Donald."

"I wasn't sure you knew, but it's Angela's birthday next Sunday," said Donald once greetings had been exchanged. "I thought perhaps the girls would want to organise something for her."

"We *didn't* know," said Dan. "Thanks, Donald."

"She doesn't usually make much fuss, you know what she's like. She'll treat it like another working day."

"I expect so," said Dan. "But I'm sure we'll do our best to make it a bit more exciting!"

Dan passed the vet's message onto his children.

Sophie shook her head. "Imagine not telling anyone it's your birthday. You wouldn't get any presents!"

Becky looked at her. "Well, *we're* certainly going to get her something. Shall I make a cake?"

"Oh yeah! Chocolate, please," said Sophie, rubbing her tummy.

"It's for Mrs Fitz, not you!" chided Becky, with a smile.

Dan rubbed his stomach too and grinned. "Chocolate's a good idea, I say. After all, I'm sure she won't eat *all* of it by herself…"

The girls and their father drove up to Tangletrees early the next morning, picking up Sophie's friend, Isabel, on the way. Everything seemed unusually quiet when they arrived, and Mrs Fitzgerald was nowhere to be seen.

"Come on, Is," said Sophie. "Let's visit Ginger and Whisky."

As the two younger girls ran off, Becky picked up Albert and turned to her dad. "Where do you think Mrs Fitz has gone?"

Dan shrugged. "Perhaps she's overslept," he said, mischievously.

They eventually found Mrs Fitzgerald sitting upstairs in her apartment on the top floor, looking half-asleep. One hand supported her head, the other clutched a cup of coffee.

"Is everything OK?" asked Dan, a little concerned.

"Not really," sighed Mrs Fitzgerald. "Those wretched dogs spent the night eating their way through their bedding! They made a terrible mess." She sighed. "They got me up at half past four this morning and I couldn't get back to sleep, so I'm ahead of myself today. I don't know how though, most of the time I was kept busy clearing up their mess!"

"I'll do Billy and friends," said Dan, sympathetically. "You carry on recovering for a bit."

Sophie and Isabel pounded up the stairs.

"Whisky and Ginger look well, don't they Mrs Fitz?" said Sophie.

Mrs Fitzgerald arched her eyebrows. "Rather too well for two dogs who decided to chew their beds rather than sleep on them last night!"

Becky told Sophie what had happened while Mrs Fitzgerald drained and rinsed her coffee cup.

"Well, enough moping," announced Mrs Fitz. "It's time for dog walking. Some serious exercise might calm down those naughty creatures."

"We'll take them!" piped up Sophie, enthusiastically.

"Oh yes, *please*, Mrs Fitzgerald," joined in Isabel. "We'll be very careful."

"I'll go too," said Becky.

"I'm afraid I can't let you three go on your own, not with those mischievous mutts!" said Mrs Fitzgerald. "But you can help me. Come on, zip up your coats and let's gather the troops."

Being outside seemed to give the spaniels even more bouncy energy. They were jumping and pulling on their leads, but poor Mrs Fitzgerald simply couldn't bring them to heel.

Although the dogs at Pet Hotel were allowed off their leads in their enclosed exercise space, Mrs Fitzgerald often took them all for a walk on the lead in the field behind the grounds of Tangletrees. Today, as the spaniels were a bit unpredictable, they were only accompanied by

Bertie, Charlie, a terrier called Spot and a mongrel called Arthur. Mrs Fitzgerald decided to do a second shift in the afternoon, weather permitting.

She was just about managing to keep the spaniels under control until they came to a rather bumpy bit of the field. One sharp tug from Whisky pulled Mrs Fitzgerald off balance. She stumbled over a furrow and the naughty dogs seized their chance. They tugged their leads out of her hands and went racing up the field.

"Whisky, Ginger!" Becky shouted, but the dogs kept running. Sitting up, Mrs Fitzgerald put her fingers to her mouth and made the most extraordinary whistle. The girls jumped, but the spaniels simply ignored her — they were much more interested in an old cattle feeder at the edge

of the snowy meadow, circling it as they chased each other.

"I'd better get them," said Mrs Fitzgerald, running up the field after the runaways. "Stay here with the other dogs, girls."

Becky, Sophie and Isabel held the other leads extra firmly and watched as Mrs Fitzgerald made her way up the field after the wayward dogs. As they saw her coming, Whisky and Ginger moved faster and faster. Mrs Fitz followed, dodging first one way, then the other, but the snow was slippery and her boots didn't grip as well as their paws. One minute she was up, the next she was down, and for the second time that week the girls saw their friend take a tumble. The incredible thing was that as soon as Mrs Fitzgerald fell the dogs stopped running and went to see what had happened.

"Are you all right, Mrs Fitz?" asked Isabel.

"It's OK girls. It's only my pride that's hurt. And

look at these two." She leaned forward from where she was sitting and grasped their leads.

"Gotcha!"

A while later, all chores done, everyone was back sitting in the kitchen at Tangletrees with hot toast and butter. Mrs Fitzgerald was passing round marmalade and home-made jams.

"I wonder why those two dogs are so disobedient?" said Becky.

"I don't think they have ever been trained," said Mrs Fitzgerald. "They're lovely animals and quite intelligent. It's a great shame no one has taken the trouble to teach them basic discipline. I'd love to have a go, but I don't think I've got the time."

"And it's not really your job," reminded Dan.

Just then, the phone rang. "If it's someone with a dog I'm going to tell them we're full up!" he joked. A short while later, Dan ducked his head back into the kitchen. "Becky, it's for you. It's Amy!"

5

Shopping With Amy

"Is it OK if my friend comes to see me here at Tangletrees, Mrs Fitz?" asked Becky. She was already planning a great afternoon with Amy at Pet Hotel, looking at the animals and showing her how she groomed Billy.

"Of course — as long as she doesn't mind energetic dogs!" laughed Mrs Fitzgerald.

"Oh, she *loves* animals," replied Becky. "She's not allowed any pets of her own, but she is looking after Crispy the hamster this holiday. It might help change her mum's mind."

"Well, we'll have to keep Whisky and Ginger hidden when her mother drops her off, then! We don't want to ruin her chances by showing how difficult pets can be!"

When Amy called round, Becky took her straight up to Mrs Fitzgerald's flat to meet everyone.

"Why don't you show your friend round," suggested Mrs Fitz when they'd said hello.

"Good plan," agreed Dan. "It looks as though it might snow again later, so if you want to spend some time outside, I'd go now."

"You'll have to watch out for Oscar the goat," giggled Sophie. "He'll eat anything!"

"And there's Billy the Shetland pony, of course!" said Becky, proudly.

"You've got a pony?" Amy asked, her eyes wide.

"He's not mine, but I spend a lot of time with him. Come on."

"I've been dying to come up here," said Amy as they walked out into the cold air. "It must be brilliant to see so many animals."

"I just love it," said Becky.

"I wish my parents could understand animals just a little bit. Even Crispy's too much for them. My mum says he gives her a headache, running around in his wheel all night!"

Becky pulled a face. "Well, she certainly wouldn't get on with Billy, then." She unbolted the stable door and showed her friend inside.

"Oh, Becky, he's so sweet. Do you ride him?"

"No he's too small for me, but I'm working on Dad to let me have lessons at Haresfield stables in the summer. Come on — you've still got to meet Oscar!"

They went across to visit the old white goat in his shed, and patted and stroked him. Oscar was so curious and taken with Amy's dark bunches that he rested his front feet on the fence to get a better look.

But as soon as Amy was close enough, Oscar grabbed her green scarf in his mouth and started to chew. Amy squealed with laughter as Becky tugged frantically on it until the goat let go.

"Only slightly chewed," she panted. "You're lucky — he prefers red ones!"

"I'll show you the cattery downstairs, now, if you like," said Becky. She paused, then added, "We're looking after Deborah Porter's cat at the moment."

Amy looked surprised and then blushed at the mention of Deborah.

"That's funny. She never sends Lady to kennels normally."

"No, I think this was an emergency."

Together the girls went down and looked in on the cats. Lady Jane allowed Amy to stroke her, but still seemed snooty when it came to Becky.

'Great,' she thought. 'Even Deborah's cat hates me!'

An hour or so later, Alice Radcliffe, the nurse from

the Haresfield vet's practice, arrived. She was bringing some supplies for the animals, and over a cup of tea, a thought struck Dan. He talked to Alice, then went to find Becky and Amy.

"Fancy a trip to town, girls? Alice is on her way there now."

"That's a wicked idea," said Becky. "Shopping! What do you think, Amy?"

Amy nodded, and the two of them dashed off to get their coats.

"Here's some money for those jeans you need," Dan said to Becky, while Alice cleared ice off the car windscreen.

"Thanks, Dad!"

Alice took them to Hockley's department store in Clayton. With Alice in tow, she and Amy wandered round the shop holding up scarfs, jackets, shirts and skirts. Becky had never been clothes shopping without her mum before and it was hard to make a decision.

"Aren't you meant to be getting jeans?" whispered Amy, as Becky tried on a very chic fur hat.

"I am, but Alice didn't hear Dad say. And there are so many things I need. Like *this*..."

"It looks really good on you. Here, look in the mirror."

It did look smart. It was black and white with a turned up brim and cost the same as a pair of jeans. Memories of Deborah's neat, expensive-looking appearance flitted through Becky's mind.

"Ooh, look at you! Is that what you want, Becky?" asked Alice brightly. "It's a bit pricey, but it's lovely, isn't it?"

Becky nodded. "It is," she answered, and followed Alice to the cashdesk. As they waited in the queue, Becky started feeling guilty. She wanted to be more like Amy's other friends, but she knew she needed jeans much more than a fur hat, no matter how nice it looked.

"I've changed my mind!" she announced suddenly, just as they got to the front of the queue. "I saw a lovely pair of jeans over there."

"That's more like it, Becks," laughed Alice. "You'd probably find one of the pets back at

Tangletrees would pinch that hat and set up home in it!"

Becky felt herself flush with embarrassment. What would Amy think of her now? But Amy just smiled as they went to look at the jeans, and complimented her on her choice. She also helped her choose a very nice purple neckscarf for Mrs Fitzgerald's birthday. Then Becky found a card with Shetland ponies on it. Having bought everything she needed, Becky felt a lot happier as they walked back to the car.

"Thanks for today, Becky," said Amy. "It's been great fun."

"Well, thank you for phoning. And for your advice on the jeans."

"They were definitely the right choice — who cares about silly hats when you get to spend every day at Pet Hotel?" said Amy, comfortingly.

Becky smiled as Alice drove carefully through the slush and ice to drop them off at their homes.

6

Escape!

When the Ashfords got to Pet Hotel the next day, Mrs Fitzgerald was once again to be found at the kitchen table, but this time she was sound asleep.

Dan leant over and touched her arm. "Angela, would you like a coffee?"

She jumped. "Oh, Dan… girls… What time is it? What a night!"

"What happened?" asked Sophie.

"Well," Mrs Fitzgerald rubbed her eyes, "dear old Whisky and Ginger decided to howl all night. They started at about eleven and the others joined in shortly after that — cats, dogs, budgies, even hamsters for all I know. I kept getting out of bed to calm them down, but they'd start up again the minute I got back to sleep. In the end I thought I may as well get up and read. Looks as though I dropped off."

Mrs Fitzgerald stood up and stretched. "Do you know, if you're tired enough, that kitchen table is quite comfortable! Oh, Lord, look at the time. I'm late with the feeds."

"*We'll* start," said Dan. "You get dressed and have some breakfast."

The spaniels were also still asleep when they got downstairs. Most of the animals perked up when the girls pulled the blinds up and started feeding them, but Becky was very worried to see that Lady didn't seem well. The Siamese was in a huddle at the back of her cage, mewing loudly. Becky went to stroke her, but the cat flinched and turned her head. The girl gulped and looked at her dad nervously.

"She'll be OK, Becky, she's just been unsettled by the noise last night," said Dan. "Lady's got three whole days to recover before Deborah comes back." Becky wanted to cry. No one understood how important it was that Deborah's family were pleased with the service at Pet Hotel.

That afternoon, Dan took Becky out on his rounds with Donald Hall. Dan went out with Donald whenever he got the chance, to pick up extra tips about treating animals. Today they were going to a farm to visit a lame horse.

Sophie and Mrs Fitzgerald stayed at home. They were having a couple of quiet hours. Mrs Fitz was writing a list of roads that should receive the leaflets about Mr Hardy, while Sophie had decided to do a drawing of Tangletrees in the snow for her mum. Every now and then there was an outburst of barking from the spaniels and Sophie went down to the basement area to check that they were all right.

"You seem to have a bit of a magic touch with those dogs," remarked Mrs Fitzgerald, as she went to answer the phone.

"Angela, it's Dan," came the voice in her ear. "The car battery has finally given up on me. Donald's already left and Becky and I are stranded in the middle of nowhere. We've had to walk twenty minutes to find a phone box and, to make things worse, I think it's starting to snow again."

"Where are you exactly?" asked Mrs Fitzgerald, scribbling down directions as he spoke. "OK, I'll get the Land Rover out. You'd better get Becky back to the car where it's warmer. I'll be with you as soon as I can! "

Sophie helped Mrs Fitzgerald load the Land Rover with chains, jump leads, rugs and a rucksack full of flasks of tea and chocolate biscuits, but with all that there wasn't much room left for Sophie. They were expecting a visit from the young vet Jake Green, at any moment, so Mrs Fitzgerald waited until he arrived and then asked if he wouldn't mind staying with Sophie for an hour.

"No problem!" he exclaimed.

Jake had come to give Mrs Fitzgerald's cats

their annual innoculations. While he went upstairs to hunt for them in the flat, Sophie went down to see the spaniels in the basement once again. The dogs jumped up in delight, pushing their muzzles through the wire of the pen.

"Hello, Ginger, Whisky, how are you doing in there?" The more Sophie tickled their noses the higher the spaniels jumped, padding up and down impatiently.

"Oh dear, you think you're going to get a walk, don't you?" She felt sorry for them, even though they had already had their daily run outside. Suddenly a tempting thought crossed her mind. *She could take them out.* She could cope. After all, Mrs Fitz had said she had the 'magic touch'.

Sophie went to put on her coat and fetch their leads, looking in on Charlie and Albert on the way. The two dogs were asleep, curled up together by the fire in the office — not at all interested in a cold walk. It was probably just as well, two dogs would be easier to handle on a quick run.

Unfortunately for Sophie, the dogs were even

more keen for some exercise than she had first thought. As soon as she opened their pen they flew past her and bounded up the stairs to the next floor.

"Oh no!" wailed Sophie as she ran after them, calling their names. Her heart was pounding. She could hear that they'd run upstairs towards the cattery. She had to get them back! Running as fast as she could along the basement corridor she flung open the back door, hoping that the sound would remind the dogs they were going out. Once they got there she would shut it, grab them and put their leads on.

The minute the door was opened, the spaniels came tearing along the corridor. As they appeared, she leaned heavily on the door to push it shut, but it was stuck on something! Close to tears now, Sophie pushed with all her strength. It had to close! Just as she budged it, three streaks of fur rushed passed her and out through the gap. *Three*?

Sophie flew after them, her anorak falling off her shoulders, but she was wearing wellies and couldn't move very fast. She soon lost sight of them and hurried to the end of the paddock. "Whisky, Ginger, come here!" she bellowed over the hedge of the meadow, but she couldn't see anything under the darkening evening sky.

Slowly, she started to walk back to the house, looking and calling all round the empty outdoor runs as she went, but there was no sight or sound of the dogs. Why had she done such a stupid thing? She was going to have to tell Jake what had happened. And who was the third animal that had escaped? Sophie hurried indoors and had a quick search round all the cat rooms. Her worst fears were confirmed. There, in the corner, was an empty, open cage.

It was Lady's.

"Sophie, what's the matter?"

On seeing the young vet, Sophie burst into tears. "Oh, Jake," she sobbed. " I've just done a terrible thing. I wanted to take the span… so I undid the… and they ran upstairs… I opened the back door… and Lady went with them… now it's dark and Becky will be so cross and…"

"Whoa!" Jake stopped her. "Hold on, Soph. I don't know what you're talking about. The only word I recognised there was Becky. Let's go into the office and sit down so you can tell me slowly."

"No, Jake! This is urgent!" Sophie tried to explain about the dogs and Lady from the beginning.

"Let me double-check things here," said Jake. "There are two dogs and a cat somewhere out there in the murk and if we don't get them back inside your life won't be worth living."

"Yes!" said Sophie in relief. "Come on. What are you waiting for?"

Now Jake was fumbling in his pockets. "I'm just looking for something which might... aha! Here it is!" Triumphantly, he held up a very thin silver whistle. The vet blew on it, but Sophie didn't hear a sound.

"That's no good, it's broken!" she cried.

"This, my dear Sophie, is a dog whistle. Humans can't hear it, but dogs can. It might bring those naughty hounds running back to us."

The pair went outside and Jake blew the

whistle again. It was eerily quiet all around the grounds.

"Come on, Soph, let's walk up to the meadow."

The two of them moved on, Sophie calling and clicking as she'd heard Mrs Fitzgerald do, Jake blowing into the dog whistle. They stopped by the meadow hedge to listen. All seemed quiet for a moment, and then from nowhere they heard the heavy sound of paws on the snowy ground and affectionate panting.

"Oh, please let it be them!" whispered Sophie.

Jake caught the two spaniels as they wriggled through the hedge and Sophie quickly slipped their leads on. "Let's get these two securely inside and find a torch," he said. "I think the cat may take a bit more persuasion to come back."

They led the two runaway dogs back to their block and Sophie fetched the torch. Then, the pair headed out into the cold early evening to look for Lady.

Jake made sure they did a very thorough search. They checked the whole meadow, including all the stables and the barn, and shone the torch on every tree they passed. But Lady was nowhere to be seen.

"I'm sorry, Soph, but there's not much more the two of us can do," said Jake. "We've been out here over an hour. It's dark and cold and she's probably hiding well out of sight, not far away. Lady knows where warmth and food is, she'll come back. Now, we'd better get in ourselves because the others will be home soon."

"I know," murmured Sophie to herself. "And I'm going to be in *so* much trouble!"

7

A Night At Tangletrees

"I hope you've cooked us a large shepherd's pie followed by apple tart and custard for pudding, Sophie," joked Dan, as the stranded motorists and their rescuer came through the front door. "Or have you spent the whole afternoon playing with those dogs?"

Sophie and Jake were standing ready to greet them, but at these words Sophie's face crumpled.

"Actually, there's been a bit of trouble this afternoon," said Jake.

Dan frowned. "You all right, Soph?"

Sophie took a deep breath and told the story as

calmly as she could. Becky could hardly believe her ears.

"You did what? Oh, Sophie, why couldn't you leave them alone? I can't believe it. You stupid, stupid girl!"

Sophie burst into tears.

"Come on, Becky, shouting's not going to help. You can see that Sophie is sorry."

"But, Dad, aren't you going to tell her off for even thinking about letting the dogs out?"

"Of course." His face darkened. "That was very irresponsible, Sophie, and I hope you've learned your lesson."

"I have, Dad, I'm sorry. I'm really sorry, Mrs Fitz, but I thought they'd be OK with me."

"All right, Sophie," said Mrs Fitzgerald. "But you must ask before taking animals out of their pens — especially such strong-willed dogs. I must admit though, I did notice earlier that the door to Lady's cage was a bit loose — I meant to ask you to look at it, Dan. Lady might have got out by herself if she was scared enough."

Now it was Becky's turn to burst into tears. "We have to go and look for her, Dad."

"What do you think, Jake? Is it worth having another look?"

"Of course!" declared Jake, standing up. "Five pairs of eyes are better than two. Have you got any more torches, Mrs Fitz?"

"Loads!"

"Then what are we waiting for? Let's give it another go!"

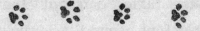

A rather tense search party left the warmth and light of the Pet Hotel and scoured the grounds around Tangletrees. It was half past seven by the time Mrs Fitzgerald and Dan decided to give up.

Jake tried to strike an optimistic note. "Let's not worry yet. Lady knows where you are. Just leave some food out and a light on and I'm sure she'll be back by morning."

"I think Jake's right, girls," said Dan. "There's nothing more we can do now. We're all tired and

hungry and I think we could use an early night."
He put a hand on Mrs Fitzgerald's shoulder. "Let's
do what the expert says and wait for tomorrow
morning."

"Look, Dan, why don't you and the girls stay
the night here? You need to get a new battery for
the car tomorrow and it would save me ferrying
you around until then. Besides, I think a sleepover
would make us all feel a bit jollier."

"And jollier still would be a sleepover with fish
and chips!" said Dan, winking at the girls.

"Oh, yes, please," said Sophie. "I'm starving!"

"And if I volunteer to go and get it, can I stay
for supper too?" asked Jake.

"Of course you can. Here, it's on me." Dan
handed Jake some money. "Come on girls — let's
get the ketchup out!"

Becky smiled, grudgingly. Being round Jake
and Mrs Fitz would help keep her mind off the
dreadful thought that Lady might not come back.

Sophie went with Jake to get the food while
Becky helped Dan and Mrs Fitzgerald feed and

check the other animals were all comfortable for the night.

On his way back down, Dan found Becky standing in front of the empty cage in the cat room staring at Lady's velvet cushion and full food bowl.

"Come on, you," he said. "I think I hear our fish and chips arriving."

Luckily, there were two spare rooms in Mrs Fitzgerald's apartment — the girls were to share the sofabed in one, while Dan had a mattress in the other. With the table cleared and the washing up done, Mrs Fitzgerald vanished upstairs to organise an astounding array of nightwear — T-shirts of all shapes and colours, striped pyjamas and some old leggings.

"This lot was going to Oxfam. Just as well I never got round to taking it!"

From amongst all the bits and pieces Becky picked up a huge white T-shirt while Sophie danced round in a tie-dyed orange and purple top.

"That was an artistic experiment that misfired!" laughed Mrs Fitzgerald. "But you look great in it, Soph. Now come along, hop into bed. It'll soon be morning at this rate."

As they didn't have toothbrushes the girls cleaned their teeth with their fingers, enjoying the flavour of Mrs Fitzgerald's different toothpaste. They washed their faces with her lavender soap and dried themselves with a big, pink fluffy towel which smelt of her cosy airing cupboard.

It was well past ten o'clock by the time they were both finished. Sleepily, the sisters went into the kitchen to say goodbye to Jake, who was just leaving.

"I'll see you soon," he said. "And don't worry. That cat'll be back in her cage before you know it."

'I hope so,' thought Becky. She and Sophie kissed their dad and Mrs Fitzgerald goodnight and then went off to their room.

Although they were both on the sofabed, Becky was glad they were sleeping in separate sleeping bags. She was still upset and annoyed with Sophie and didn't feel like sharing the bedclothes with her. But after lying in the dark for ten minutes or so, Becky heard sniffing.

"Becky, I'm really sorry about Lady. I feel so awful — I know you're all really cross with me."

Becky couldn't bear the sadness in her sister's voice. "It's OK, Soph, I'm sorry too. And Mrs Fitz knows you didn't mean any harm. Why don't we get up really early and go out looking for Lady together before the others get up?"

"OK. Whoever wakes up first wakes the other one."

"It's a deal. As long as Whisky and Ginger don't get us all up first!"

In the silence, the two girls wriggled their sleeping bags towards each other and snuggled together. It wasn't long before they both fell into a deep sleep. So deep that they didn't hear Dan come in and kiss them goodnight, or feel Bertie make a little nest between the warmth of their resting bodies.

Outside, big snowflakes were falling thick and fast — covering everything at Tangletrees Pet Hotel in a layer of glistening white.

8

Search In The Snow

The girls were so tired they slept right through till breakfast time. Smells of hot toast and coffee wafted along to their room. Once they heard the bacon sizzling they quickly got dressed and hurried along to the kitchen.

It had been snowing heavily all night. They could see no paths, no gates, no familiar bushes, just mounds and mounds of white snow. Somehow it didn't look quite as beautiful as it had done on the first morning of half-term.

"Morning, girls!" beamed Mrs Fitzgerald.

"Morning. Wow! I'm starving!" said Becky.

"Well, I think we've got a hard day ahead of us and an English breakfast is always a good way to start things off."

"Where's Dad?" asked Sophie.

"I'm here!" Dan peered round the kitchen door. "I've been out with the shovel, checking on Billy and Oscar. It's a wilderness out there."

"I don't suppose you've found Lady, have you?" asked Becky in a small voice.

"No, love. I'm sorry." He took off his boots and closed the door.

"We'll start searching straight after the morning feeds," promised Mrs Fitzgerald. "In fact, after breakfast, why don't you two go out while I see to the indoor animals."

"Good idea," said Sophie, through a mouthful of bacon.

"I wanted to be out there by now, but I couldn't get up this morning," said Becky. "I was in such a deep sleep I didn't even hear the spaniels."

"No, me neither," replied Mrs Fitzgerald.

"Perhaps they've guessed their training starts today!"

"You mean you're going to take them on after all?" asked Sophie.

"They've been so much trouble," grumbled Mrs Fitz, "that I really don't think I have any choice!"

It was hard work trudging through the snow in the meadow. The drifts were higher than the girls' wellies in places and it wasn't long before their feet were squelching inside their boots.

"Might as well take my wellies off," said Sophie. "My feet can't get any wetter than they already are!"

As she sat down in the snow, Mrs Fitzgerald appeared, adorned in her full winter garb, the spaniels in tow. "Your dad's braved the roads in the Land Rover to get a new battery," she said. "No luck with Lady, then?"

Both girls shook their heads sadly. "And I've got soaking wet feet," said Sophie, miserably.

"I'm not surprised. By the look of your tracks

you've searched all over the place."

"If only it hadn't snowed last night we could've tried to find Lady's paw prints," said Sophie, helplessly.

Becky felt too fed up to make conversation. With every minute that passed she lost further hope of ever finding the Siamese. And, guiltily, she realised she was just as worried about what Deborah Porter would say to her as she was about what might've happened to poor Lady Jane.

"The snow out here is much deeper than I thought," said Mrs Fitzgerald. "No training for you two today, you lucky hounds." But the dogs weren't listening. Even though they found walking in the snow difficult, they were still pulling on their leads.

"Look out, you'll have me over in a minute."

"Mrs Fitz!" said Sophie. "I think they can smell something. Look!"

Sophie was right. Both dogs had their heads up and were sniffing the air.

"They seem to want to go towards the old

shelter in the corner," said Mrs Fitzgerald. The dogs gave another sharp tug on their harnesses. "Oh no you don't," she said, twisting the leads tightly in her hands. "I'm keeping a very firm hold on you, this time. Come on, girls, let's see what's got them going."

They made their way towards the shelter in silence. As they got nearer, Becky stopped.

"Listen!" she whispered. Through the cold, still air came a very distant mewing. "Mrs Fitz, it's Lady!" she said, and started to run forward.

"Hang on Becky. That shelter isn't safe any more, remember, and Lady may be trapped."

But Becky dashed over. The others followed as quickly as they could, Whisky and Ginger sniffing more urgently with every step.

When Becky got to the shelter, she stopped to listen to where the noise was coming from. It *did* look dangerous. The wooden sides had already given way and the glass roof panels were smashed and broken. Becky crouched down and peered inside. There, in a dark but dry corner, were two large blue eyes peering back at her.

"She's here!" cried Becky. "Quick! Let's get her out."

Mrs Fitzgerald bent down alongside Becky. "Thank goodness. Now this is going to be tricky. I don't think we can reach her without touching the wood and risking the whole lot crashing down."

Sophie joined them. "*I* could," she said. "I'm small enough. I could crawl in a little way on my tummy without touching anything."

Mrs Fitzgerald looked doubtful. "You'll have to grasp her firmly or we'll lose her again. I don't think you'd better, Soph."

"Yes, remember what happened last time you thought you could do something," snapped Becky, a little unkindly.

"*Please*, let me try," pleaded Sophie.

Lady's mewing seemed to get louder and more desperate.

"Oh, let her, Mrs Fitz," said Becky, whose heart was beating fast. "We mustn't lose Lady again!"

Mrs Fitzgerald breathed deeply and puffed out

her cheeks. "OK. But let me move these two out of the way and, whatever you do, *don't* touch the structure. Sophie, this is important. If you don't think you can do it, stop and come back."

The spaniels had been standing patiently and went obediently with Mrs Fitzgerald as she moved several metres away. There must have been something in her tone of voice that told them that this was not a time to mess about.

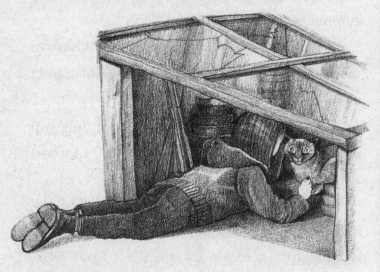

Sophie dropped to the ground. Although there was no snow under the collapsed roof, the ground was frozen hard and she could feel the cold through her anorak. She gently wriggled towards the cat with one arm outstretched, murmuring encouraging things all the time. Becky was crouched behind her, every nerve on edge.

Just as Sophie reached Lady, the cat decided to bolt. She ran straight into Becky's arms. With a cry, Becky grabbed her and stood up.

"Well done, girls!" cried Mrs Fitz.

"Here." Sophie unwound her scarf. "Let's put this round her."

"Take my scarf as well, Sophie," said Mrs Fitzgerald, and Sophie held the warm clothes over Lady as they headed for the house.

"She's shaking," said Becky, her own voice trembling.

"Yes, but she's alive," replied Sophie.

Becky looked at her sister and the relief in her dark eyes.

"Take her up to the kitchen while I put these two away," yelled Mrs Fitz. The girls hadn't realised the old lady could move so quickly before. She had the dogs in their pen and was upstairs within seconds of their own arrival in the kitchen. "Put her on the rug next to the range and shut the door. We must get her warm."

Becky placed Lady on the rug beside Mrs Fitzgerald's old stove, while she bent down to examine Lady calmly.

"Will she be all right, Mrs Fitz?" asked Becky, gently stroking the cold, damp bundle of fur.

"I hope so, dear. You two keep talking to her and I'll pop into the bathroom and get a towel. I think we'll phone the vet's. My big moggies could survive that cold, but this poor creature is a little more delicate."

The girls cuddled Lady and she mewed occasionally. She was too weak to resist their attention and just watched them intently. When Mrs Fitzgerald appeared with a warm towel they gently rubbed the cat's cold body.

"Hey, girls, listen!" Mrs Fitz bent down and stopped them moving their arms. Lady was purring loudly. "Well, that sounds encouraging. And Donald is on his way."

The vet seemed to take for ever. Mr Hall eventually arrived to find the Siamese curled up asleep on Becky's lap. He checked her very thoroughly, but couldn't find anything wrong.

"I think she's suffering from shock as much as anything," he said. "She just needs warmth, little portions of good food and lots of love for a few days, then she'll be right as rain." Donald smiled at Becky. "She couldn't be in a better place!"

He handed the limp little cat back to her, then sat down in the rocking chair. "Jake told me about your lively dogs, Angela."

"Very ill-disciplined if you ask me. They belong to the Hardys. Sophie and I are so fed up with them we're going to try to teach them the basics."

"Hardy? Isn't he the chap who wants to turn the land opposite into some kind of leisure park?"

"Yes, he's the one. Which reminds me, we ought to start leafleting the roads around here and get some sort of petition going. We really must do it this week, girls. You'll support us, won't you, Donald?"

"Of course. Unfortunately, that James Hardy's rich and very determined. We're going to have our work cut out," Donald said, draining his teacup. "Anyway, I'd best be getting back to my own little cat. Poor Rosie, she won't go outside at *all* in the snow!"

After Mr Hall had left, Sophie sneaked off to check on her beloved spaniels while Becky stayed by the stove stroking Lady, who purred contentedly. She closed her eyes and prayed that they could get the little Siamese fit and well again before Deborah collected her...

9

The Porters' Return

Dan decided the girls had waited long enough for their skating trip. Straight after feeding the animals at Tangletrees they got in the car — starting much better with its new battery — and headed off to Clayton, picking up Amy and Isabel on the way.

"Isn't it funny," laughed Sophie. "We're going to an artificial rink when there's all this real ice around!"

Sophie and Becky had only ever skated once before so they weren't very good. Isabel had never been at all, but when they got there, Amy turned out to be a bit of an expert.

"I've been coming here since I was five," she

told Becky, who was clinging to her for support. "My mum skated for the county."

"Wow! What a brilliant mum!"

"Yes, but she doesn't like pets!" Amy laughed and shook Becky's rigid arms. "Come on. *Relax!*"

Becky soon started to get the hang of it and eventually plucked up enough courage to let go of Amy for a moment to wave to her dad, who was happily sitting down at the side of the rink, watching them. The two younger girls were a long way behind, giggling and clinging to each other.

When she held Amy's hand, Becky felt much more confident. They started whizzing round the rink until Amy suddenly made her stop.

"There's Kadisha and Holly! Let's go and say hi."

Becky felt her heart sink. Kadisha and Holly were really good friends with Deborah. "I'll wait here for you," she mumbled, gliding to the slide.

"No, come on. Please, Becky."

Becky took Amy's hand again. She didn't want to ruin her new friendship by being awkward.

Within moments Amy and her friends were

busy chatting about what they'd been up to.

"I'm having a great half-term, thanks to Becky here," announced Amy, grinning. "We've been shopping, I've been up to see Pet Hotel — it's brilliant! And now her dad's brought us here."

"Oh, Tangletrees Pet Hotel," said Holly, looking Amy's new friend up and down. "Did you know Deborah came back yesterday evening? She phoned me and said she was going to pick up Lady Jane this afternoon."

Becky was speechless with horror, but tried not to let it show.

"Well, she'll be happy to see just how well Lady has been looked after," said Amy confidently. "See you next week." With that, she dragged Becky off.

Becky could barely move. She'd told Amy the story of Lady's rescue in the car. "Why did you say that? I'm not sure if Lady's ready to go home, yet."

"Don't worry, Becky. I bet Deborah will be so pleased to see Lady…" But Amy's voice trailed off.

They continued to skate round in silence. Even when Dan finally braved the ice and had the others in hysterics with his falls and cries of pretend horror, she could barely raise a smile.

As the group were going back to the car, Becky told Dan that Deborah would be round that afternoon.

"Well, Lady seems much better, now. Home would probably be the best place for her."

"But do we need to tell them what happened?"

"I'm sorry, Becks. We can't let something like that happen to one of our guests without telling the owner. I think most people would appreciate our honesty."

Becky knew what he meant, but still felt sick to her stomach. She was just going to have to make sure she kept out of sight when Deborah arrived that afternoon.

After dropping Amy home, the Ashfords met Jake just leaving Tangletrees with his instrument bag.

"What, no broken ankles?" he asked in mock disbelief. "I'm disappointed with you!"

"We were brilliant!" said Dan. "Did Angela call you out?"

"Yes. It seems Lady's owners are coming to pick her up early, and Mrs Fitz just wanted one of us to give her a once over."

"And how is she?" asked Becky, anxiously.

"Fit as a fiddle and ready to go," said Jake. "She's eating healthily and reacting well to people, now. The owners should be perfectly satisfied. See you tomorrow, folks!"

Despite Jake's upbeat report, Becky's heart still leapt when the doorbell chimed a couple of hours later.

"I expect that's Mrs Porter," said Mrs Fitzgerald.

"I'll go," announced Dan. "Coming, Becks?"

Becky looked at her father, horrified.

"Listen, Becks, I don't want to force you to do anything, but you'll have to face her sooner or later. Why not now, here, where you're comfortable? Besides, Deborah will probably like the fact you've taken such a personal interest in her pet."

Becky wanted to believe him, but as Dan

opened the front door, she could feel her confidence fading. Mrs Porter and Deborah looked their usual bossy selves, and Deborah walked straight past Becky without a glance.

There were no words of polite greeting. "We've come for Deborah's cat," said Mrs Porter, primly. "I trust there have been no problems?"

"Lady is in fine shape, Mrs Porter, but I have to confess there has been a bit of an incident I think you ought to know about..." Dan ushered Mrs Porter into the office. After fixing Becky with a scowl, Deborah followed her mother.

Becky stood in the office doorway while Dan told mother and daughter what had happened, her hands in her pockets and fists clenched, digging her nails into her palms. Lady was in her basket on the desk, curled up contentedly.

"*But*," concluded Dan, "I am delighted to say that Lady has made an excellent recovery. The vet checked her this morning and says she seems stronger than ever. Isn't that right, Becky?"

Becky nodded.

Mrs Porter drew in a long breath, her face grave. "Well, I'd like to inspect Lady straight away, and I can tell you here and now that we will not be calling on the services of Pet Hotel a second time."

Dan ignored her statement and started to open the basket. Deborah walked forward to help.

"Lady, pretty Lady," she cooed, lifting her out. "How are you, you poor, poor pusskins?" Becky was impressed to see that Lady looked overjoyed to be back with Deborah.

Mrs Porter peered over and looked at the Siamese. "She certainly does look well."

"Mummy!" said Deborah. "Her fur's so silky and she's purring so loudly. I'd almost forgotten how beautiful she is!"

"Well, if you think she's all right, my darling, I suppose we'd better pay and leave. It's just as well we came home early. I mean, *really*…"

Dan and Mrs Porter leant over the desk to discuss money and Deborah started to put Lady back in her basket. Taking a deep breath, Becky went to help.

"She's very pretty," said Becky.

"Yes, she is," said Deborah, gently coaxing Lady into the basket. "Thank you," she added.

"It's nice to have a pet that loves you so much. I've got a dog, called Albert, and I would feel awful if anything ever happened to him. I tell him everything, he's like a best friend." She paused. "Amy told me how important Lady is to you."

"*Amy*?" asked Deborah.

"Yes, she's been over a couple of times. She knows all about what happened."

"Isn't she looking after the class hamster this

half-term?"

"Yeah. She's trying to convince her mother she should have a pet, but even though Crispy is lovely, I don't think she's had much luck."

"She should try a cat like Lady, or a dog, maybe."

Becky nodded, then Deborah picked up the basket and followed her mother out of the office. Dan shook hands with Mrs Porter.

"Well, thank you for letting us look after Lady. Again, I'm so sorry about what happened, but I'm sure you'll find her none the worse for wear."

"Thank you, Mr Ashford. We'll let you know if we notice anything untoward. Come along, Deborah."

As they opened the door the group met Sophie, Isabel and Mrs Fitzgerald holding Whisky and Ginger.

"Hello!" said Dan. "Mrs Porter, meet Mrs Fitzgerald, the owner of Tangletrees, my youngest daughter, Sophie, and her friend Isabel."

Becky was livid with them for appearing with the dogs at that moment and stood back to wait for the bouncing and yelping round Lady's basket.

But it didn't happen. The dogs did go up to the basket, but calmly and gently, tails wagging, noses snuffling. It was almost as though they were saying farewell to an old friend.

"We're just beginning some training," said Mrs Fitzgerald.

"What delightful dogs!" said Mrs Porter. "They hardly look as though they need training."

"I'm afraid it was these two that caused all the trouble," said Dan.

"How extraordinary!" whispered Mrs Porter, backing off slightly. "They seem very well behaved now. Goodbye everyone, and er... thank you." With that, she bundled her daughter towards the car.

"There you are, Becky!" said Dan, closing the door. "That wasn't so bad, was it?"

Becky had to admit that things seemed to have gone fairly well. But the real test for her would be what Deborah told the others back at school.

10

Happy Birthday Mrs Fitz

There were two reasons to be cheerful at Pet Hotel — the Hardys were coming to collect Whisky and Ginger, and it was Mrs Fitzgerald's birthday!

Becky and Dan had made a cake the night before and on Sunday morning the girls set about icing it. It was chocolate, of course, and they seemed to have got chocolate butter icing on every single gadget in the kitchen, not to mention most of Sophie's face.

After the cake was more or less finished and all Mrs Fitz's presents were wrapped, Becky and Sophie hid the goodies carefully in the boot of the car. They drove towards Tangletrees through the melting slush, Dan taking care to drive carefully round the corners.

It was fairly late in the morning when they joined Mrs Fitzgerald. She had already done the morning feeds and was outside in the meadow, checking the fence.

A chorus of 'Happy Birthday!' greeted her across the field.

"Good morning, everyone!" she cried. "How on earth did you know it was my birthday?"

"We've got spies!" laughed Sophie, reaching up to give Mrs Fitzgerald a kiss.

"Oh, have you now? Well, I think that's quite enough attention for me, why not give some to Billy, instead."

Becky and Sophie ran off to Billy's stable, Bertie and Charlie trotting along behind them.

"I can't wait to give Mrs Fitz her pressies," said Sophie. "I love birthdays!" Then, she sighed. "Isn't it a shame the snow has melted so fast?" The green fields of Haresfield were rapidly returning.

"Well..." said Becky. "Since we lost Lady, I've gone off the snow!"

The girls led Billy out into his field so he could trot about and nibble at the sodden grass. Bertie and Charlie squelched happily about at his feet.

"I shall miss those spaniels, you know," said Sophie. "It's been brilliant helping Mrs Fitz with their training."

"Well, Mr Hardy had better be grateful."

Becky was interrupted by her name being called across the meadow. She turned and saw Amy running up to meet them.

"Hope you don't mind me coming over," she puffed. "Mum dropped me off while she takes Gran to church, and guess what she told me in the car — I can get my own hamster!"

"Amy, that's brilliant!" said Becky, beaming.

"Looking after Crispy did the trick! I proved I can care for my own pet! We're going to get one next weekend. Why don't you come with us?"

"I'd love to. Thanks!"

The girls left Billy grazing in his field and

started to walk back to the house.

"By the way," said Amy, "Deborah phoned me."

Becky carried on walking, her hands in her pockets, staring at the ground.

"She's really pleased to have Lady back, and says pusskins has never looked better in spite of what happened. She didn't say anything nasty about Tangletrees — in fact, she mentioned how nice you'd been about Lady."

Becky wasn't sure what to say. "Oh that's brilliant! Thanks for telling me, Amy."

Amy smiled. "She wants to come up and have a proper look round herself some time, and I said I'd ask you."

"Why not?" said Becky, breathing out an enormous sigh of relief.

The girls were so excited about giving Mrs Fitzgerald her presents that the day seemed to drag by. After Amy had gone home, Becky and Sophie spent most of the afternoon sweeping the runs and cleaning the cattery.

Eventually, at four o'clock on the dot, Mr Hardy's big grey Rolls Royce pulled into the drive.

"Go and get the little dears, Sophie," ordered Mrs Fitzgerald, a twinkle in her eye.

While Mrs Hardy stayed in the car, Mr Hardy knocked on the door.

Becky answered. "Hello, Mr Hardy," she said, politely. "Your dogs are out in the meadow. This way!"

Mr Hardy followed her through the reception and outside, past the dog runs at the back of Pet Hotel.

"Call their names, Mr Hardy!" Mrs Fitzgerald instructed.

As they heard his call, two very excited spaniels dashed across the grass to meet him.

"Hello, my beauties!" he said, stroking and petting them as they ran around, clearly overjoyed to see him. Mr Hardy turned to Dan. "I hope they haven't been much bother."

"Well, Mr Hardy," spoke up Dan, "I think I'd

better let Mrs Fitzgerald do the talking. Here she comes now." As Mrs Fitzgerald came over, the girls saw her tighten her lips.

"I can't say everything started very well, but I think we've got a happy ending," she said, airily. "I'm afraid to say your dogs have been two of the most badly behaved animals I have ever known. They even managed to chase a rather sensitive cat outside into temperatures of minus five degrees."

Mr Hardy looked horrified. "I did wonder whether they would miss us."

"I don't think it was much to do with missing you, Mr Hardy, I think it was more to do with the fact they have never been trained how to behave. Sophie and I have now given them an intensive schooling session and we are very pleased with the results. I hope you will be too."

Mr Hardy smiled at her despite her harsh tone. "I was most impressed by the fact they came when I called their names. I'm not sure they've ever done that first time before!"

Twice the Trouble

"That's just for starters," said Mrs Fitzgerald. "Whisky! Ginger! Heel." And the dogs ran to her side. "Come on Sophie, let's put them through their paces."

Together, they went through all the exercises the dogs had learnt. Everything went splendidly until they got to the one Sophie called, 'The Glove Trick'. She walked round the meadow with them off their leads, and dropped one of her gloves without them noticing. After walking on for a moment she then turned to the dogs and said, "Seek back!"

The dogs ran off to find the glove, and everyone thought they'd got the idea — but suddenly they were distracted.

Mrs Hardy, curious to see what was going on, had got out of the car and taken the outside route to the meadow. Whisky and Ginger lost their concentration and headed off to say hello, but as they reached her a tractor drove past in the lane outside. Quick as a flash, the spaniels jumped over the fence and started to chase the noisy vehicle.

Sophie ran after them as far as the gate, calling their names. Mrs Hardy shrieked, while Becky watched through her fingers. Mrs Fitzgerald was grimly silent.

"Wait here, Soph," Dan shouted. "I'll get them!" He followed the dogs into the road.

By now, everyone had joined Sophie at the gate to watch. Whisky and Ginger were running all over the place, and Dan was slowing down. He had seen a car coming the other way and knew that somehow he had to stop an accident. He waved and waved at the tractor driver who eventually caught sight of him in his mirror, and thought quickly. The driver swerved across the road, totally blocking it, then leant on his horn. The car ahead stopped just in time, and the dogs were still trying to find a way past the tractor before Dan grabbed their collars.

"*Sorry*!" shouted Dan to the farmer. "Thank you. I thought they were finished."

"You want to keep them under control!" yelled the driver. "Crazy dogs!"

Twice the Trouble

The man in the car waved at Dan and did a mock wipe of his brow. It was Jake Green.

Dan gratefully took the dogs back to the gate and the tractor went on its way. Jake turned into the drive.

Mr Hardy led the others in a round of applause as Dan brought the two dogs back in. "You rescued our babies!" cried Mrs Hardy. "How can we thank you enough?"

"Yes, thank you," said Mr Hardy, shaking Dan warmly by the hand. "I'm so sorry these two have caused you so much trouble."

Dan frowned, a little embarrassed. "Well, *I'm*

sorry our demonstration went a little —"

"Oh, not at all, that was just bad luck," said Mr Hardy, waving away Dan's apology. "Mrs Fitzgerald, would you consider continuing with their training?"

"Well, that's flattering of you to ask," said Mrs Fitzgerald. "But this latest incident has only demonstrated that they'd be better off with a real expert."

"No, no, I'm sure that was just a hiccup. You're quite right, of course, they've never been properly trained. To see them behaving so well…" His face was flushed with delight. "Get them in the car, Harriet, and I'll go and sort out the bill."

Mrs Hardy attached the leads to their collars and led the naughty pair carefully back up to the car as Sophie and Becky waved goodbye.

As Mrs Fitzgerald took Mr Hardy into the office, he couldn't help but notice her undelivered leaflets lying in a pile on the desk.

"You know, Mrs Fitzgerald," he said. "If you've got the time I'd love to look round the rest of the place before I leave."

Mrs Fitzgerald raised an eyebrow. "It would be a pleasure, Mr Hardy. We'll start on this floor."

She gave him a thorough tour, pointing out every detail and explaining how everything at Tangletrees Pet Hotel worked, as well as their hopes and plans for the future. They ended up back in the meadow, standing opposite the dilapidated old shelter. Mr Hardy, who had been fairly silent throughout the tour, at last turned to Mrs Fitzgerald and cleared his throat.

"Mrs Fitzgerald, we really should have spoken before now. I'm afraid I may have distressed you by publishing my plans for the leisure complex."

"Well, as you see, I am ready to fight you every inch of the way," said Mrs Fitzgerald, smiling broadly.

"I have been very impressed with what I've seen and I think — in consultation with you — I should rethink my plans."

"What do you mean?" asked Mrs Fitzgerald, suspiciously.

"Well, I think perhaps I should consider other sites. I could also make a better local investment here." He smiled at her puzzled face. "An investment in terms of a small donation to a wonderfully run Pet Hotel that is doing such splendid work."

"Well, Mr Hardy..." spluttered Mrs Fitzgerald. "I mean... that is extremely generous of you..." Her voice trailed off, her face beaming.

"Well, how would you like a new shed? This old thing looks a bit dangerous to me. If you don't mind, I'll send a couple of men over first thing tomorrow to take it down. Think of it as payment for the training sessions." He smiled. "And I'm sure there must be one or two other projects round here you could use some help with?"

"I am thrilled, Mr Hardy," said Mrs Fitzgerald, reeling. "I really don't know what to say! Just wait till I tell the others!"

"Yes, well, I must get back to my carload. Let's go and break the good news together, shall we?"

"What took you so long?" asked Dan when

they arrived back at Mr Hardy's Rolls Royce.

"Mrs Fitzgerald has some news for you," said Mr Hardy as he climbed into his car. "Thanks again. I'll see you very soon!" Shutting the door with a cheery wave he drove off.

"What did he mean, 'see you very soon'?" asked Dan, as Jake, Becky and Sophie joined them.

"I have just had the best birthday present ever!" beamed Mrs Fitzgerald. When she told them what Mr Hardy had said, Dan gave a cheer, the girls kissed her for a second time that day and Jake hugged her so hard her feet came off the ground.

Once things had finally calmed down and Donald and Alice had arrived, Becky and Sophie managed to bundle them all into the kitchen, where they made tea and brought out the cake. Mrs Fitzgerald couldn't stop smiling, opening her presents with delight.

"Becky this scarf is wonderful...Thank you

Dan, how clever of you to get my favourite wine... and Sophie, what can I say!" Mrs Fitz held up a pair of lilac gloves. "These gloves are quite... something!"

"I knew you'd like them," said Sophie, happily.

"And thank you all for such a fabulous birthday feast. More cake, anyone?"

Everyone had seconds, and Dan poured out more tea.

"I still can't believe it," sighed Mrs Fitzgerald, as she slid the last slice on to her plate. "I'd turned James Hardy into such a monster in my mind, and he really is quite nice!"

"Shame you had all those leaflets printed," said Dan, winking at Becky and Sophie.

"They served their purpose!" replied Mrs Fitzgerald, smiling. "A small donation will be so useful for repairs and the like!"

"That's boring!" moaned Sophie.

"Why not put it towards building a whole new stable block, so that we can take more horses!" suggested Becky, excitedly.

"Or towards soundproofing the dog block!" offered Dan, chuckling.

"Whatever we do with it," Mrs Fitzgerald said, "I'm just pleased we're not facing a leisure centre on our doorstep any more!"

"Hear, hear!" agreed Donald, as Alice nodded too. "And that extra cash will help make Pet Hotel better than ever."

Dan stood up and stretched. "Meanwhile, there's school tomorrow. Sorry to break up the party, Angela, but I should get this lot home."

"Of course. Jake will help me do the evening rounds, won't you?"

"I'd be honoured!" said Jake, bowing.

"And two new guests are due about now," she

continued.

"Oh yes," said Dan. "I'd quite forgotten!"

"I hope we haven't missed the door in our excitement," fussed Mrs Fitzgerald. But then, right on cue, the doorbell rang. The Pet Hotel team could hear yapping and barking on the doorstep, so Sophie ran to the window to have a look.

"It should be the Greshams with their two dogs, I think. Well, Sophie?" asked Dan.

Sophie turned back to the room, grinning. "Yes. And guess what Dad? They're both spaniels!"

Mrs Fitz buried her head in her hands.

Dan laughed. "Remember what we decided — Pet Hotel is open to anyone and anything. Even *spaniels*!"

"Thank you for reminding me," said Mrs Fitzgerald as the others all laughed. "Well, come on girls — let's get them in!"

Animal Casebook

It's so important to teach your dog how to be obedient —
otherwise it can get itself, and you, in all kinds of trouble!
Properly-trained, your dog will always obey your commands
and never be a nuisance at home or in public places. Dogs are
'pack' animals. In the wild they like to live in groups. Each pack
has a top dog or leader. Your family soon becomes your pet's
'pack' and by training it you become its leader. Your dog is
really a wolf in your living room!

Training is all about kindness and patience. Dogs need
plenty of time to learn. Sometimes they'd much rather be
playing than training, just like you!

Getting Started

Begin training with your dog as early as possible — puppies
don't pick up bad habits that way. **No** is the first word a dog has
to learn. That way it soon starts to realise when it's being good.

Always start your training with your dog on its lead. That
way you are still in control.

Nobody likes being shouted at and your dog feels just the same.
Keep your voice gentle and pleasant, but firm. Your dog will
respond to the tone of your voice. Try and vary it for each
command so that it knows what it's meant to do. Shrieking at
your spaniel won't get you anywhere. Dogs aren't fools, they'll
simply ignore you!

Well-trained dogs should be able to follow six basic commands:

- **Heel**
- **Sit**
- **Stay**
- **Wait**
- **Come**
- **Down**

Try teaching your dog one command at a time.

Teaching a dog to *sit* is really useful. A simple way is to tell it to *sit* each time you offer it a meal. Say *sit* in a clear voice and gently press its hindquarters to the floor. Make it wait for a minute or so and then give him or her its meal. When you say *right* it's allowed to eat. Gentle, repeated training works wonders.

Getting a dog to *come* to you isn't too hard either. Bend down and move slowly backwards calling your pet to you all the time. Use one word of command like *come* or *here*. Try not to confuse your dog with too many instructions. A treat or lots of praise helps encourage it to *come* to you. Always reward your pet when it does well.

TOP TRAINING TIP

Lots of praise works wonders. Let your dog know you're happy when it does well. You like gold stars, your dog does too!

DON'T FORGET:

Training your dog should be fun for *both* of you!

Perfect Puppies

Having a new puppy can be a lot of fun, but it's also a big responsibility. It's very important that you train your dog to behave well right from the start. Well-trained puppies grow to be loving, obedient companions – your best friend!

Some dogs can be really naughty and not do what they're told. Some are just stubborn, but sometimes there are medical reasons why pups can't pick up their training quickly. A puppy with sore hips may not like to run about much and will stay put rather than *come* to you. If your pup seems always a bit naughty or unhappy have a word with the vet. Most problems can be worked out quite easily.

Have you ever been invited to a puppy party? They're great fun. Young, vaccinated pups all meet up together and learn to get on with each other. Mixing with other dogs or 'socialising' is a very important part of a young dog's education. The puppies learn basic training and all the owners are taught simple aspects of dog care like worming and keeping their pets' teeth healthy and clean. Your local vet may well run Puppy Parties.

Clever Creatures

Did you know that some dogs can be trained to save lives? For three hundred years, St Bernard dogs in the Alps were used to find and rescue travellers who had got into trouble on the snowy mountainside. The powerful dogs worked in a team of four. Two of the dogs kept the victim warm, while a third licked his face. The fourth dog went to get help!

Siamese
If You Please

Siamese cats definitely stand apart from the normal moggie, they're athletic and aristocratic looking with gorgeous sapphire blue eyes. The Siamese is Britain's most popular 'foreign cat' and no wonder — they're beautiful. Siamese cats are big attention seekers and impossible to ignore. They are great 'talkers' with loud voices. You don't own a Siamese, it owns *you*!

Did You Know?

● Siamese cats are first mentioned in the *Cat Book of Poems* which were written about six hundred years ago. That's some pedigree!

● Siam was the old name for Thailand, where these lovely cats come from.

● Expect to pay a fair bit for a Siamese kitten, often around two hundred pounds. Some champion cats are worth many hundreds even thousands of pounds because they have won many cat shows and have a prestigious pedigree.

● There are four classic Siamese cats: the Seal Point, Blue Point, Chocolate Point and Lilac Point. Points are the extremities of the body, the feet, ears, face and tail.

● Siamese kittens are born white with no points at all. Shame!

● Siamese cats often live well into their teens. That means they would survive to well over a hundred if they were human!

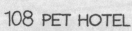

Have you read all the

PET HOTEL

books?

1

WELCOME TO

Pet Hotel

Sophie and Becky are both pet crazy – so when
they move to Sussex and meet their new
childminder, they're in for a sensational surprise.

Mrs Fitzgerald lives in a huge house with a host
of wonderful pets. The sisters quickly find
themselves walking dogs, feeding goats and
grooming Shetland ponies. But Mrs Fitzgerald's
love of animals doesn't stop there: she's a
lady with plans, *big* plans!

3

The Non-Stop Runaway

A Norfolk terrier is checked in and everyone takes an instant shine to her. But Sophie and Becky are warned that Pickle isn't the dream guest she appears to be.

The new arrival's got the wander-bug – she simply can't resist running away. The wayward dog's escape acts are now so famous no other kennels will even take her on. But the problems only start for Pet Hotel when it's time for the terrier to go home!

4

Pet Hotel Detectives

Sophie and Becky are delighted when their first exotic pet comes to the stay at the Hotel – Myriad, a beautiful Blue and Gold Macaw.

Yet the visit turns sour when a sleepover at Tangletrees is interrupted by a midnight break-in! In horror, the team discover that the Macaw's cage has been smashed, the bird nowhere to be seen. Can the sisters track down the thieves before it's too late for Myriad?

More animal-packed Pet Hotel books available from BBC Worldwide Ltd

The prices shown below were correct at the time of going to press. However BBC Worldwide Ltd reserve the right to show new retail prices on covers which may differ from those previously advertised in the text or elsewhere.

All BBC titles and a free catalogue
are available by post from:

Book Service By Post,
PO Box 29, Douglas, Isle of Man, IM99 1BQ

Credit cards accepted.
Please telephone 01624 675137 or fax 01624 670923.
Internet http://www.bookpost.co.uk
or e-mail: bookshop@enterprise.net for details.

Free postage and packaging in the UK.
Overseas customers: allow £1 per book (paperback)
and £3 per book (hardback).